'What do you think you'll be when you grow up dear?' asked me when I was just a chick, with my grey fluffy fea webbed feet.

Gully as a chick, dreaming of being a pop star...

Cornwall is full of artists...

How many times have *you* been asked that? And what do you say? A crane driver, postman or footballer, fireman or popstar? Do you know what I told my mum? I told her that ever since I was an egg, all I've ever wanted to be is a seagull.

So here I am, and I'm a *really* good seagull too, and do all the things I'm expected to do, like pinching ice creams and pasties from small children and dive bombing old grannies in nice hats, and generally making a huge nuisance of myself all over the village what with all my squawking and splattting. Oh yes, I'm a top gull.

In fact, I'd go as far as to say I'm *the* top gull, and let's face it, the seaside wouldn't be the same without me!

But you know, sometimes, just sometimes, I wonder whether I could have been anything else, and the other day when I did a huge splattt in the shape of a crab, and a *fantastic* crab at that, I wondered whether I couldn't be an artist.

It can't be that hard, can it? Cornwall is full of them. Take our village. There are more strange and peculiar looking artists and painters and sculptors than there are fishermen or boat builders or fish sellers.

I suppose you've all seen graffiti art before, where people spray boring bits of wall or railway carriages with fantastic murals from spray paint cans? Well I do the same here by doing graffiti splattts on anything or anyone that I think is

He always beeps his horn as loudly
as he can as he passes poor
Mrs Baker's cottage...

a bit plain or boring. I call it *gulffiti…*

So, if you're plain or boring, watch out!

Now take my least favourite family, the Trumpers, for instance. Lionel Trumper, with his nasty back-to-front baseball cap and big, bulbous, bloated belly with its filthy, fluffy belly button, drives a great big monster of a car with huge tyres and a giant chrome bumper. It is a horrible car, and it is Lionel's pride and joy.

Lionel calls it 'the beast cruiser,' and loves to keep it sparkling clean, and he polishes it every day, and when he arrives in our village, he always beeps his horn as loudly as he can as he passes poor Mrs Baker's cottage. It makes her old windows rattle and her false teeth drop out and her spectacles shatter. Then he parks it right in the middle of the road outside her little cottage, right in everyone's way, and (and this is the good bit) right under the gullery where the princess and I live.

I *love* to splattt on it. Every day. A bit of gulffiti makes the beast cruiser look more interesting, and even better it makes Lionel absolutely furious with rage.

Take last Sunday for instance. Lionel had just finished polishing the beast cruiser's roof, and Honeysuckle was bringing him out a mug of tea with fifteen spoonfuls of sugar in it, in an attempt to make him a sweeter person. She was, as usual, singing (though the singing was not as sweet as the tea!).

Lionel's tea and biscuits arrive

'Here we are, my love,' she said. *'I like a nice cup of tea in the morning, Just to start the day you see, And around about eleven my idea of heaven is a nice cup of tea…'*

'Do shut up, my love. You squawks worse than them gulls,' said Lionel.

'And there's biscuits. Digestives…' she said.

'Chocolate digestives?' enquired Lionel.

'Uh, no. Ordinary. That's all they had my love…'

'I don't do ordinary biscuits, my love. I only does chocolate. Bourbons, gypsy creams, mega double choc chip choco muffins smothered in chocolate with chocolate flakes sprinkled on, anything chocolate will do. Try and get it right for once,' he said, throwing the digestive up into the air like a Frisbee.

The digestive biscuit spun up towards the gullery, where I was sitting with the princess, out of sight of the Trumpers. I caught it, and snapped it in half with my beak, and we shared it, half each.

'What happened to that biscuit?' Lionel said. 'I never even heard it land…'

Thanks Lionel. Like you, we prefer chocolate biscuits, but we're not that fussy, me and the princess. I peeped over the edge of the gullery, down onto the roof of the beast cruiser. It was very shiny and sparkling, and gleaming and clean; spotless in fact.

We can't have that, can we?

I waited for Lionel to pop inside for a second. When he did, I backed up to the edge of the gullery, and stuck my tail out over the guttering and over the street and splattted right onto the blank canvas of the beast cruiser's roof. I turned and looked down at my piece of work.

It was an interesting piece of gulffiti. It looked rather like waves washing over rocks, and splashing up to make a spray, and there was what looked like a fishing boat in the background. I can't say it was one of my best ever creations, but it was ok.

Lionel didn't think so though!

'Aaagh! I can't believe it!' he screamed. 'I just cleaned that! Every time I cleans it one of them flying rats does a splattt on it…'

Steady now Lionel, I don't like this flying rat business. It's very rude of you.

'Filthy things. Every time….all polished and smart, the beast cruiser, then they do this. Its disgustin'! Its almost like they're up there…watching me…waiting until I finished cleaning it so they can do this…'

Yep. Got it in one Lionel!

It was an interesting piece of gulffiti

Tyrone, alarmed by the noise that his father Lionel was making, leaned out of his upstairs bedroom window. He looked down onto the roof of the beast cruiser.

'Wow, dad! That's brilliant,' he said. 'It looks like waves splashing onto rocks, and there's a fishing boat in the background. Those gulls aren't so stupid after all!'

Well, thank you Tyrone. It's nice to be appreciated.

Of course, gulffiti is not the only art that I like to do. I have a leaning towards modern sculpture.

Now this is quite a hard thing to explain to you all, but by what I can see from some of the art galleries in my village, modern sculpture means that you pick up any old piece of rubbish and stand it up on its own for people to gawp at. Then those people, obviously not wanting to look stupid, have to look at the piece of rubbish and say that they know what it is meant to be. Do you know, I'm only a gull, but I'm sure that most of the time they don't *really* know.

Anyway, for years now I've been trying to make a success of this modern sculpture, and like a proper artist I've been spreading and arranging bits of rubbish all over the streets for people to look at and admire, and to say what they think it is meant to be.

And do you know what they say? They say 'Look at the rubbish! It's disgustin'! Where's the bin men, why aren't they clearing up? It's all over the road! There'll be rats!' and silly remarks like that.

This is art!

Rubbish? Disgustin'? Clear it up? How dare you…this is *art*!

Then last week, I finally began to get somewhere.

In my village there is an artist called Boris. He leaves me out grilled mackerel fillets on his windowsill sometimes, still sizzling in the grill pan and cooling nicely in the fresh sea breeze. At least, I think he leaves them out for me, so I always take one anyway, and he doesn't seem to mind….

Actually, Boris is such a mad artist and so away with the fairies that he doesn't even realise if I've pinched one, and that's the way that modern artists are. Boris is always too busy in his gallery, arranging some piece of junk or another on a plinth, to be counting the mackerel fillets in his grill pan.

Lionel, who has more money than sense, thinks that Boris' modern art is marvellous, and goes into Boris' art gallery and spends lots of money on junk, sorry, I mean on Boris' art. I don't mind because I quite like Boris.

On the Monday evening, the day after I'd **splatttered** the beast cruiser, Lionel put a bin liner full of rubbish outside his cottage. At dawn the following morning, a time when it is usually safe to go down into the street, I popped down from the gullery to have a peep at what he had thrown out. I slit the bin liner open with my beak and looked inside.

Boris and one of his barmy paintings

13

I picked out an egg box, a mouldy orange and a baked bean can. In the middle of the road, I placed the bean can on top of the egg box and the mouldy orange on top of the bean can. I stood back and admired my sculpture. Shall we call it my *gullpture*? Well, whatever we call it, it looked fantastic anyway.

But as is the way with us gulls, I had an overwhelming need to see what else there was inside that bin liner. I was not disappointed.

Three greasy bacon rinds, half a fish finger, a fried egg so hard that it was like a rubber one you can buy from a joke shop, some chips, a raspberry yoghurt that had spilled over everything else, a piece of rock hard cheese, some empty cans of Sabre the hell hound's dog food and, can you believe it, a nearly full packet of digestive biscuits. There was no chocolate though. Lionel had eaten all the chocolate.

Anyway, what I couldn't eat there and then, I carried up to the princess for breakfast, and what she didn't want I left all over the road, with all the other wrappers and plastic containers and cling film and papers and lids and stuff.

Don't ask me why I did that. I'm a gull, right? Its what I do.

Far from expecting a big fuss when Lionel awoke later on, I expected a few gasps of admiration for my fabulous gullpture.

'Oh my…whatever is this? Filthy animals! We got foxes or dogs or cats or rats or something!' shouted Lionel. 'Quick love! You'll have to get down here and clear it up! It's terrible! It's all over the road!'

Honeysuckle came to the attic window and leaned out. 'What is it my love? I'm trying to clear all this junk out of the attic. It's really dusty in here. Whatever is all the fuss?' she sneezed.

'Whatever
is all the
fuss?'
she sneezed.

Lionel stood in the street and pointed at all the garbage strewn everywhere.

'You'll have to bring down the broom, my love, and your apron and rubber gloves, and get down on your hands and knees and scrub up all the filth,' he said.

'What will you be doing then, my love?' she asked.

'I got a phone call to make my love. An important one. To the council. About foxes and cats and dogs and all manner of vermin,' said Lionel.

Mrs Baker had been woken up by all the fuss and was looking out of her door.

'Excuse me,' she said. 'But if you leave bags of rubbish out, the seagulls open them and eat the scraps and make a mess.'

'That's all I need. A mad old woman telling me that some thicko gull is clever enough to undo bin bags with it's beak!' said Lionel. 'Oi, and mind your door against the side of the beast cruiser. I just polished it!'

Poor Mrs Baker went back inside.

Honeysuckle began to sing as she swept the street. *'My old man's a dustman, he wears a dustman's cap, he wears cor blimey trousers, and he lives…'*

'Do give it a rest my love,' said Lionel. 'This has made me feel quite poorly, and your singing is making it worse.'

And Honeysuckle didn't even notice as she swept up the egg box, bean can and orange into a pan.

My wonderful gullpture…gone forever…consigned to the dustbin…

On that same evening, Lionel once again put out a bin liner full of rubbish, and once again as dawn broke I flew down from the gullery to see what goodies I could find in there.

I split the bag open and put my head right in. I pulled out three old plastic flowers, a cracked mug with a picture of the queen on it, and an old tea caddy with 'East, west, home's best…' written on it. Honeysuckle had cleared the old junk out of the attic.

I put the tea caddy into the middle of the street, and placed the cracked mug with the picture of the queen on top of it. I took the plastic flowers, firstly the pink, then the blue, and finally the faded orangey yellowy one, and arranged them beautifully in the mug.

I took a step back. If I say so myself, I had made a marvellous gullpture out of some old junk, and I felt very proud.

So good did I feel that it brought on hunger pangs. What a feast the Trumpers had left today inside that bag. There was so much to choose from that I grabbed the bin liner with my beak and tipped it up and emptied all the fabulous contents completely on the street…just so that I could see exactly what was on offer for breakfast today, that's all.

Breakfast? This was a banquet!

Breakfast? This was a banquet!

For starters, I opted for two sardines that had been left in a can and smothered in banana custard, followed by a large gala pork pie and some blancmange, and then for afters, a burnt beefburger with rice on it, garnished with some boiled cabbage.

I flew up to the gullery with half a nasty pasty and two ring doughnuts for the princess…but sadly she was still asleep, bless her, so I had to try and scoff the lot. I have to say that the nasty pasty was just too much, so I ate the rather sticky sweet doughnuts and left the nasty pasty in the gullery for later on.

It's tough work being a gull, but someone's got to do it!

I felt even more proud when who should walk past at that early hour of the morning than Boris, the modern artist. Boris couldn't sleep. He was looking for what artists call inspiration.

What he found was my gullpture and ..er… a street strewn full of garbage.

When he got to my piece of work, my gullpture, my art, he stopped. His jaw dropped.

He stood back in Lionel's doorway and looked at it. He crossed the street and looked at it from the other side.

Boris got down on his hands and knees and crawled towards it through all the tins and wrappers and mouldy old bits of food. Bits of broken biscuits and yoghurt and squashed fish finger stuck to both his knees, but Boris didn't seem to notice. He cocked his head to the right, then to the left, and stared at my gullpture.

'Wow, man,' was all he could say. 'Wow…'

Boris looked around, up, and then down the street. He bent over and picked up my gullpture and held it up. I peered down at him from the gullery. I made a little quiet squawk and he looked up at me, carefully holding the gullpture. He put his finger to his lips and whispered 'Shh…' and winked at me. I winked back. He skipped off down the quiet street carrying the gullpture with him.

A little later I heard Lionel come out of his cottage door and crunch out onto all the rubbish in the street.
'Oh my lord, my love! Quick! You must get out here with the broom! They've been here again, them cats or foxes or bears have been at the bins again…Honeysuckle! Quick love!' he shouted.
  'But how can it be bears, my love? This is Cornwall…' she said, rushing out with the broom.

'My love, we're in the countryside here. Strange things happen. Now please get sweeping,' said Lionel, pulling a banana skin from between his fat toes. 'I feel very stressed. I have to take a walk.'

Lionel waddled off down the street and out of sight.

"Wow. man."
was all he
could say. "Wow..."

EAST, WEST,
HOMES BEST.

My mate Boris' gallery

I sat back down in the gullery, only after a few seconds to be greeted with the unmistakeably delicious whiff of grilled mackerel fillets drifting across the village rooftops. I sniffed the air. Irresistible.

Boris is so kind. He must be preparing a little snack for me!

I flapped into the air and glided low across the slate rooftops to Boris' art gallery, and landed on the wall opposite that looked right in through the big front window. There he was, carefully arranging the plastic flowers in the cracked mug with the picture of the queen on it, pink in the middle, blue on the left, orangey yellowy on the right, on top of the old tea caddy, and now all on a plinth amidst all his other arty sculptures. Boris stood back with a big grin on his face.

He reached forward and put a price tag on my gullpture. Now I can't read all that well, but I swear it said 'Memories - £250'. Nice name for it Boris; wish I'd thought of that!

The only thing remaining was for Boris to find someone extremely stupid to give him £250 for it. Someone so utterly brainless and clueless that it almost defied belief. Someone who couldn't even put his baseball cap on the right way round. Someone whose name almost escapes me…

He came blubbering up the street like a walking sack full of blancmange. He blubbered past the wall on which I was perched. He blubbered into Boris' gallery, and blundered into a chair put there for customers. Lionel's bottom was so huge that it only just squashed in. It was as though he was wearing the chair.

'Boris,' he said. 'I'm depressed. There's bears and hyenas and jackals coming to the bins at night and chucking garbage all over the street, and Honeysuckle takes so long to clear it up. Between you and me, she don't do a very good job…but I'd like to buy a little something to cheer us up…'

Boris stepped aside, revealing the plinth with the plastic flowers and mug and tea caddy.

'Its my latest creation,' he said.

Fibber, Boris. It's my gullpture.

'I call it 'Memories',' he said. 'I think its very special.'

Lionel sat open mouthed, wedged into the chair. 'It is special Boris,' he said. 'It is a most marvellous work of art, and I am a good judge mind. How much?'

'£250.'

'That is too cheap, Boris, for a piece of work like that.'

'£300?' ventured Boris.

'Look,' said Lionel, whose stupidity was breathtaking, 'I got plenty of money. Tons of it. Shall we say £350, no, £400?'

'Well, if you really think so,' said Boris.

'I do, Boris. You're very talented,' said Lionel, getting up and lifting the chair as he did so.

He tried to get at the roll of £20 notes in his pocket, but couldn't, and Boris had to pull the chair away from his bottom like a cork out of a champagne bottle. Lionel handed the roll of £20 notes to Boris, picked up the gullpture and blubbered out the door, down the street and off back to his cottage.

You may be thinking to yourself, 'Yes Gully, but what about the grilled mackerel cooling on the windowsill at the back of Boris' gallery?' Quite. Do you know, I had almost forgotten.

Almost, but not completely.

I took off and flew over the roof, down to the windowsill, and there they were, all in a row; rich, oily and still sizzling a little, but not enough to burn my beak. I landed on the edge of the grill pan and began the feast. Well, it *was* quite some time now since my breakfast banquet.

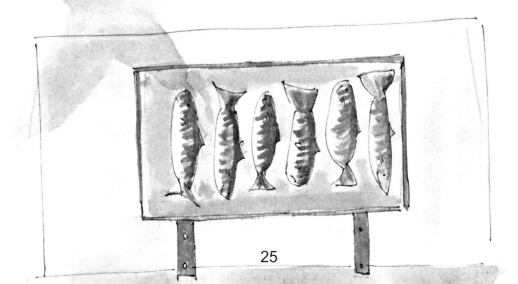

Well. it was quite some time now
since my breakfast banquet.

Then a strange thing happened. Just as I was thinking that I should be going, and maybe leave Boris one or two mackerel fillets for his lunch, he came into the kitchen and looked out at me through the window.

Instead of banging on the glass or shouting at me to get lost or calling me a flying rat like Lionel does, Boris put his thumbs up and waved a big wedge of £20 notes around and shouted 'Whoopee! Thanks Gully!' Then he buttered a piece of bread (I hate margarine) and came out to the windowsill and put it on the pan with the mackerel that were left.

'There you go Gully,' he said. 'Grilled mackerel is not the same without a piece of bread and butter. Thanks for the sculpture!'

I would have carried some back for the princess but, you know, she was probably still asleep.

So I ate it all!

It's what I do, ok?

You won't forget this in a hurry!

Shortly after I flew back to the gullery, and sure enough there she was, the princess, asleep and looking radiant. All, however, was not so peaceful down in the street.

'What have you been digging in the bins for?' said Honeysuckle.

'What are you talking about?' said Lionel, holding the gullpture aloft and admiring it. 'This, my love, is a piece of art, a sculpture by Boris, my famous artist friend. It's worth £400. Tomorrow it'll be worth £500, and the day after that, well, who knows? It's called 'Memories'. It's priceless my love'

'I chucked that old junk out of the attic yesterday,' she said. 'I'll give you memories! Here…'

Honeysuckle clonked Lionel across his fat head with the broom.

'You won't forget this in a hurry. Priceless indeed!'

'Ouch!!' shouted Lionel, and he dropped the gullpture, and she swept it into the bin with the rest of the rubbish.

Lionel sat on the step rubbing his head, and Honeysuckle went inside slamming the door behind her.

It was very funny, but I was rather upset that the gullpture had been ruined. Perhaps I'm not really cut out to be an artist!

Anyway, I'm not one to kick a man when he's down, but with Lionel it is a bit different. I picked up the half of the nasty pasty that was still up in the gullery and leaned over the parapet and looked down.

Do you know, it was the first time that I had ever seen Lionel's head with nothing on it, for the ghastly back-to-front baseball cap had been knocked off by Honeysuckle's broom. Somehow, to have nothing on his head simply wasn't Lionel!

So to oblige, I dropped the half nasty pasty down, splattt on top of him. Needless to say, Lionel wasn't too pleased, but it did look better than his stupid baseball cap, and at least the nasty pasty was on the right way around!

I strolled back to the princess. She was still asleep, bless her. She opened one eye and smiled at me. I wished that I hadn't been so greedy and that I'd saved her that fillet of mackerel...still, I know that she would understand.

You see, we're gulls, it's what we do...

Lionel and me and the nasty pasty

The End

Also available

Three mischievous adventures of the wicked seagull on CD

The range of Gully story books

Visit the website for more details

www.thegullery.co.uk

Or phone The Gullery on 01208 880937

The Author

The creator, author and illustrator
of Gully, Jon Cleave, lives in the
heart of the lovely old Cornish
fishing village of Port Isaac with
his wife Caroline and boys Jakes,
George and Theo.... oh yes, and
hundreds and hundreds
of squealing, squawking,
screaming seagulls!